KB020921

# Arthur's
# Mystery Envelope

ISBN 978-89-5605-673-9  14740

Longtail Books

For my wonderful editor, Maria Modugno,

who really knows how to polish Arthur's star

# Chapter 1

The **cafeteria** at Lakewood Elementary was filled with kids eating lunch. Some of them had brought sandwiches from home. The rest were eating school lunches. Today's choices **feature**d a mystery meat covered in gravy.★

A few teachers **wander**ed between the tables trying to **keep** the noise **under control**.

"Let's keep it down," said Mr. Ratburn. He shook his head. "I don't think anyone's listening."

---

★ **gravy** 그레이비. 고기를 익힐 때 나온 육즙에 밀가루 등을 넣어 만든 소스.

Miss Sweetwater **nod**ded. "Or maybe they just can't hear us," she said.

At one of the middle tables, Arthur and his friends were finishing up.

Arthur was **poking** at his food with a fork. "Even without the gravy," he said, "we'd have no idea where this came from."

"Ready for action, boys?" Francine asked.

"Ready," said Arthur. He **put aside** his **tray**. "And waiting," said Buster.

They started a game of milk hockey. Francine and Sue Ellen **made up** one team. Arthur and Buster were the other. They used a **crush**ed milk **carton** as a puck,★ hitting it **back and forth** the **length** of the table.

Francine **dodge**d left and **flip**ped the carton past Arthur's hand. Buster tried to stop it, but the puck **slid** past him off the table.

★**puck** 퍽. 아이스하키 경기에서 사용하는 작은 원반 모양의 공.

"Goal!" said Muffy. She was the official **scorekeeper**.

Francine smiled. "That didn't take long," she said.

Arthur **flex**ed his hands. "We just take a little while to **warm up**."

"All right," said Sue Ellen. "Let us know when you're nice and **toasty**."

"Maybe we'll need a **substitution**," said Buster. He turned to Binky Barnes. "Do you want a turn?"

"No," said Binky, crushing another carton with his **fist**. He just liked making pucks.

*"**Attention**, please!"*

Miss Tingley, the school **secretary**, was speaking over the **loudspeaker**.

*"Arthur Read, please **report** to **Principal** Haney's office **immediately**."*

A **hush** fell over the room. Everyone was **staring** at Arthur. Buster's mouth was wide

open. Binky's hand had **frozen** in mid-crush.

"Uh-oh!" said Francine.

"**I'll say**," said Muffy.

Sue Ellen just shook her head.

"You're in real trouble now, Arthur," said Buster. Sometimes Mr. Haney **yell**ed at him for running through the halls. But he had been to the *office* only once—for putting **sneezing** powder on Mr. Ratburn's desk.

"Are you all right, Arthur?" Francine asked.

"I-I guess."

"He doesn't look all right," said Sue Ellen. "He looks like one of those **deer** you read about. The ones who stare into the car headlights."

"He's in shock," said Binky. "He**'s** not **used to** visiting the principal's office. I could get there **blindfold**ed with one hand **tied** behind my back."

"What did you do, Arthur?" asked Francine.

Arthur shook his head. "I don't know. Nothing that I can think of."

Binky **snort**ed. "Don't **bother** trying that **excuse** on Mr. Haney. It never works for me."

Arthur stood up. "Well, I guess I should go."

"Nice knowing you, Arthur," said Francine.

"Good luck," said Buster. "And if you're not planning to finish those potatoes . . ." He pointed to Arthur's **plate**.

Arthur slid over his tray. "**Help yourself**," he said. "I just lost my **appetite**."

When Arthur got back to the classroom, his friends **rush**ed to his side.

"You **survive**d!" said Buster.

"With no **obvious** signs of **torture**," Binky added. He looked a little **disappoint**ed.

"What happened?" asked Francine.

Arthur **let out** a **sigh**. "Mr. Haney gave me this." He held up a large brown **envelope**. "He said it was for my mom."

"That's it?" asked Muffy. She reached out for a closer look. "What does it say? Is it **seal**ed?"

Francine **grab**bed the envelope. "It's sealed, all right." She held it up to the light. "And too **thick** to read through."

"Give it a shake," said Buster, **cock**ing his ears.

Francine shook the envelope for a moment. It **rustle**d softly. "That doesn't tell us much," she said.

Binky **fold**ed his arms. "Let's just open it."

"I can't," said Arthur. "It's **address**ed to my mother. And look what's **stamp**ed on it: PRIVATE and CONFIDENTIAL."

"That's a bad sign," said Buster. "Good news is never private."

"Besides," said Binky, "you can't start making **excuse**s until you know what kind of trouble you're in."

"Didn't Mr. Haney give you any **clue**s at all?" Francine asked.

"He said it was important," said Arthur,

taking back the envelope. "That was about it."

"If it was good news," said Muffy, "Mr. Haney would have told you. My mother always tells me right away if we've gotten a new **limousine** or if the cook is making a special **dessert** for dinner."

"He didn't say anything like that," Arthur **admit**ted.

"That means it's bad news," said Francine. "The question is, how bad is it?"

This was not a question Arthur wanted to think about.

Binky laughed. "Oooooh! I'll **bet** you lost a library book."

"I don't think Mr. Haney gets **involve**d with **overdue** library books," said Arthur. "Besides, I just returned all mine."

"Oh, no!" said Francine.

"What?" said Muffy.

"Tell us," said Buster.

"Tell me!" said Arthur.

"**Never mind**," said Francine. "It's too **terrible** to think about."

Arthur turned **pale**. "That's why you have to tell me."

"All right," said Francine. "But you **force**d me into it." She **shudder**ed. "What if you didn't pass Mr. Ratburn's **history** test?"

Arthur **frown**ed. The big test had been the week before. It had been a hard one.

"Remember, Arthur? You told me **afterward** that you wrote how the Pilgrims* came to America in 1620."

"Francine, the Pilgrims *did* come to America in 1620."

She looked **surprise**d. "Really?"

Everyone else **nod**ded.

"Well, still . . ." Francine **tap**ped the

---

★**Pilgrims** 1620년에 신앙의 자유를 위해 메이플라워호를 타고 영국에서 미국으로 건너가 매사추세츠주 플리머스에 정착한 청교도.

envelope. "The **proof** is right here. And if you failed that test, you might fail the whole year. You know what that means: summer school."

Arthur sat down in his chair and thought about his **fate**. Summer school. Perhaps the two most **dread**ed words in the English language.

*He saw himself **chain**ed to the wall of a dark **dungeon**. Outside the **bar**red window, he could hear his friends playing. He looked out through the bars. Buster and the Brain were setting up a tent for camping. Muffy and Prunella were Rollerblading.*

*Arthur looked around his **cell**. He was alone— with only some thick, **dusty** books for **company**. Then the **guard**, Mr. Ratburn, walked in. He was **slurp**ing ice cream from a cone. A few drops fell on the stones, just beyond Arthur's reach.*

"**Snap out of it**, Arthur!" said Buster.

Arthur looked at his friend **blank**ly.

PRIVATE
CONFIDENTIAL

"You know what they say," Buster went on. "Those who don't learn their history are **doom**ed to repeat it."

Arthur sighed. History or not, he felt doomed **for sure**.

# Chapter 3

Arthur could have taken the **envelope** straight home after school. But he didn't.

"Mr. Haney didn't say anything about *when* you should **deliver** the envelope," the Brain had told him. "Under international law, you have the **right** to make a plan."

They were sitting in a **booth** at the Sugar Bowl. Buster and Francine were there, too. Prunella and Muffy were **seat**ed behind them.

Arthur had bought some candy, but he wasn't eating it. He was just moving it around in front of him. The candy was **shape**d in a

**rectangle** with a big question mark inside it.

The Brain was **staring** hard at Arthur's envelope. "If only I could use X-ray **vision** . . . ," he said.

Buster **grab**bed the envelope from him. "We have to **take action**! I don't want to **spend** all summer doing fun **stuff** without you." He pushed the envelope toward the **edge** of the table. "Hey, what if you **accidental**ly lost it?"

He **shove**d the envelope onto the floor.

"It could **end up** in the **trash**. Or a **shredder**. Then **bulldoze**d into a **landfill**. Only the **seagull**s would read it there. And we don't have to worry what they think."

"That's true," said Arthur.

Prunella picked up the envelope.

"Don't listen to him, Arthur. He doesn't **look ahead**. You need to think of something that won't be **blam**ed on you in the end." She **paused**. "Maybe you could hide it in the

**laundry** basket—and it could get *washed.*" She picked up the envelope and held it carefully as if it were wet and **drip**ping. "She won't be able to read it, but you won't be blamed."

"Laundry," said Arthur. "Interesting."

"Not interesting," said Muffy. "**Risky**. You need to get it as far away from your house as possible. Buy it a first-class ticket to Alaska★ or Timbuktu.*"

"I don't have that kind of money," said Arthur.

He looked at the clock. It was time to go home.

Everyone went outside.

Francine was still **frown**ing. "There must be some way out of this," she said.

The Brain looked down at the storm **drain**.

---

★ **Alaska** 알래스카. 미국 북서부에 위치한 주(州).

✱ **Timbuktu** 팀북투. 아프리카 말리(Mali)의 북부에 위치한 도시로, 아주 멀리 떨어진 곳을 일컬을 때 흔히 사용된다.

THE SUGAR BOWL

"You could drop it in here," he said. "The **current** would carry it into Bear Lake and from there to the Otter River. Once it was in the **harbor**, it would be carried out to sea—maybe even to Europe. When it **eventually** washed up on **shore**, it's possible a mother might find it. But she probably wouldn't understand English, so you'd be safe."

"Europe is far away," said Arthur.

Francine **pluck**ed the envelope from the Brain's hand. "Don't do it, Arthur," she said. "If you try to lose it, you'll be in double trouble—for losing it *and* for whatever you did **in the first place**."

She handed the envelope back to him.

"The whole thing doesn't seem **fair**," said Arthur. "I didn't do anything! I'll just have to give the envelope to my mother and see what happens."

He had hoped saying that would make

him feel better. It didn't.

"That's a **last resort**," said the Brain. "But, of course, the choice is yours."

"Hello!" Arthur called out softly.

No one was in the kitchen except his dog, Pal. Arthur knew his mother was home, though. Her car was in the **driveway**.

"But she could be busy," he told Pal. "In fact, I'm sure of it. She could be working or helping D.W. or taking care of baby Kate. I don't want to **disturb** her."

Pal **bark**ed.

"Are you hungry?" said Arthur.

Pal **wag**ged his tail.

Arthur put down his **backpack** on the

counter. One corner of Mr. Haney's **envelope** was **stick**ing **out** of the **flap**. Then he began **rinsing** out Pal's food dish.

"Mr. Haney told me the envelope was for Mom," Arthur explained to Pal. "But he didn't say what was in it."

Pal barked.

"No," said Arthur, "I can't eat the envelope."

Pal barked again.

"No, I can't **bury** it in the **backyard**, either."

He put the empty dish on the floor. Pal **whine**d with **disappoint**ment.

"All my friends think the news must be bad," Arthur went on.

Pal continued to whine.

"Francine thinks I failed Mr. Ratburn's **history** test. She says I'll have to go to summer school." Arthur **made a face**.

Pal jumped up and down at his side.

Arthur **fetch**ed the dog food from the

**pantry**. "Maybe I'll just leave it out and not say anything. Mr. Haney said I should bring it home to her. He didn't say I **actually** had to *give* it to her. Maybe she won't even **notice** it."

Arthur **laid** the dish on the table, then opened his backpack. He **remove**d the envelope carefully and put it on the table.

"What's that?"

Arthur **whirl**ed around to find his sister D.W. standing in the **doorway**.

"What's what?"

D.W. pointed. "The envelope, **silly**."

"Nothing!" he **shout**ed. He **lean**ed on the table. "It's just a **dumb** old envelope. People could walk by this envelope for weeks and not even notice it. And even if they did notice it, they wouldn't **bother** to open a **boring** envelope like this."

"That's a lot of nothing," said D.W. "You sure are acting **weird**."

"I'm not acting weird," said Arthur. He **straighten**ed up and **fold**ed his arms. "I'm worried. I mean, I'm not worried. I'm hurried. That's it. Hurried. Third grade is very busy."

D.W. climbed onto a chair and **stare**d into Arthur's eyes. "You don't **fool** me," she said. "I know *worry* when I see it."

Arthur **blink**ed. "You do?"

D.W. **nod**ded. "Yup.★ You get **wrinkle**s."

"I do?"

She nodded. "I'm not **surprise**d. You could worry about lots of things. Like maybe someday you'll be too old for birthday presents. Or maybe you think there really is a boogeyman,✳ and he's just waiting for the first night you **forget** to check under your bed."

---

★ **Yup** 'yes'의 구어체. 응, 그럼.
✳ **boogeyman** 못된 아이를 데려간다는 귀신.

PRIVATE
CONFIDENTIAL

Arthur **sigh**ed. "Those are **regular** worries. Everyday worries. I can **handle** those."

D.W. gave him a careful look. "You mean there's *more?* **Come on**, **spill the beans**."

"All right, all right!" said Arthur. "The **principal** just gave me this envelope for Mom. That's all. Now leave me alone!"

But D.W. wasn't finished yet. She took a look at the envelope. "What are these words?" she asked.

"Which words?"

"These big words on the front."

"PRIVATE and CONFIDENTIAL."

D.W. **frown**ed. "I know PRIVATE. What does CON-FI-DEN-TEE-UL mean?"

Arthur sighed. "That only Mom can look at it."

D.W.'s eyes opened wide. She got down from the chair and **skip**ped toward the hall, singing,

*"Arthur's in trouble,*
*Arthur's in trouble."*

**For once** Arthur didn't **argue** with her. He knew she was right.

The good news was that D.W. suddenly stopped singing. The bad news was that she stopped because she had **bump**ed into her mother.

"Slow down, sweetie. We can't **afford** to put a **traffic light** in here."

Mrs. Read gave D.W. a quick kiss. Her hands were full of papers.

"What a day! If I had two heads and four hands, I'd still be behind."

Mrs. Read was an **accountant**. She always got a little **frazzled** at **tax** time.

"Mom, Arthur's acting a little **weird**. He brought home a—"

"Hey!" said Arthur. "That's none of your—"

"**Hush**, Arthur!" said his mother. "Not now, D.W. I've got a few calls to make."

She put her papers down on the **counter**.

"Arthur, what is this?"

Arthur **cringe**d. "That?"

"Yes, that." She pointed to the **envelope** and Pal's dish beside it. "On the table."

"The table? Here? In the kitchen?"

His mother **fold**ed her arms. "Yes, the kitchen table. Since when does Pal eat there?"

Arthur **let out** a deep **breath**.

"He doesn't."

"Then why did you leave his dish on the table?" She put it down on the floor. "**Honestly**, Arthur, I **expect** you to be more careful."

PAL
PRIVATE
CONFIDENTIAL

While Arthur **fidget**ed, Mrs. Read picked up the phone and **dial**ed a number. She left a message with the **secretary**.

"That's my third try this afternoon. That man is just impossible to reach." She **glance**d at Arthur. "Is everything all right? You look a little **pale**."

"Of course," said Arthur. "I was just thinking about, um . . . setting the table for dinner." He pulled out some forks and knives from a **drawer** and began placing them in front of each chair.

"Mail call!*" said Mr. Read, arriving with a **bundle** of letters. He dropped them on top of Arthur's envelope.

"How is everyone today?"

"Dear, you have **whip**ped cream behind your ear."

---

★ **mail call** 군대에서 대원들의 우편물을 배포할 때 하는 말.

"Really? I thought I had cleaned it all up."
He **scrape**d the cream off with his finger. "I
was **experiment**ing with a new **dessert**."

Mr. Read was very busy with his **catering**
business.*

"I hope no one was hurt," said Mrs. Read.

Mr. Read **sigh**ed. "Only the **piecrust** didn't
**survive**."

The phone rang.

"I'll get it," said Mrs. Read. She picked up
the mail and the envelope as she answered
the phone. "Hello? Oh, hi, Leah."

She started to look through the mail.

One letter went into the **wastebasket**.

"No, no, I'm not disappointed you called. I
was just expecting to hear from Herb."

She **put** a **bill aside** for later.

---

★ **catering business** 음식 출장 서비스 사업. 파티나 각종 행사를 위해 음식 및
테이블, 의자 등을 고객의 가정이나 특정 장소로 출장 서비스하는 사업.

"I needed some **paperwork** from him."

She **flip**ped through a **magazine**.

"Yes, I know. It's all **due** Monday."

Arthur watched his mother with an **increasing** sense of **doom**. He **edge**d his way to the door. His mother had reached Mr. Haney's envelope.

Suddenly the water on the **stove** began **bubbling** over.

"Oh, I've got to run," said Mrs. Read. "Talk to you later, Leah." She **hung up** the phone and dropped the envelope on the edge of the counter. She turned back to the stove.

The envelope **teeter**ed for a moment—and then fell into the wastebasket.

Arthur **slump**ed with **relief**. He was **innocent**. He hadn't put the envelope in the **trash**. Some other hand had **guide**d it there. It was **fate**. It was **destiny**. It was meant to be.

# Chapter 6

Dinner was hard to **swallow**. How could Arthur **concentrate** on eating? Every time he looked up, he saw the **envelope peek**ing at him from the **wastebasket**.

Even the fact that they were having hamburgers and potato puffs* hadn't **cheer**ed him up. His partly eaten hamburger sat on the **edge** of his **plate** like a **crescent** moon. Usually he **pile**d the potato puffs into a castle wall and then lined up the green **bean**s like

---

★ **potato puff** 감자튀김. 감자를 으깨어 일정 모양을 만든 후 기름에 튀겨낸 음식.

**alligator**s in the **moat**. But tonight he had only **stamp**ed the puffs and beans down with his fork. They looked like little **shred**ded carpets.

"Are you trying to save **wear and tear** on your teeth, Arthur?" asked his mother.

Arthur looked **confuse**d.

She pointed to his plate. "All that **mash**ing. You still have to eat them, you know. We don't want to waste food."

Arthur took a small **bite**.

His father **help**ed **himself** to some salad. "You're **awful**ly quiet tonight, Arthur," he said.

Arthur **squirm**ed in his chair. "We worked hard in school today." He looked at his father. "When you were in school, were tests important?"

"Oh, yes. We didn't have all the different projects you kids have today. Sometimes a single test could be half our whole grade."

"That much?"

His father smiled. "**Definite**ly. I wouldn't say you kids have it easy, but you do have more choices."

"Most important," said Mrs. Read, "we want you to do your best."

"I always do my best," said D.W., who was **swap**ping potato puffs with Kate. "It's all part of my plan."

"What plan is that, sweetie?" asked her mother.

"Her plan for world **domination**," said Arthur.

"Arrrthur!" said his father.

"Sorry." Arthur changed the subject. "Do you think every part of school is important? I mean, don't some parts **matter** more than others?"

Mr. Read shook his head. "That's hard to say. At your age I never planned on having a **catering** business. And even though my business is food, I still need to know math for planning and how to write for **advertising**."

"What about, um, history?" said Arthur. "That wouldn't matter so much, would it?"

"History's important, too," said his father. "I might want to study old **recipe**s or **create** a **meal** with some **historical theme**."

"I see," said Arthur, wishing he didn't. "It **makes sense** to learn about everything," said his mother. "You can't tell when it might come in **handy** later on." She looked down the table. "Arthur, pass me the potato puffs, please."

Arthur picked up the **bowl**.

D.W. smiled. "Arthur, isn't there anything else you'd like to give Mom **while you're at it**?"

Arthur just **barely** kept himself from kicking D.W. under the table. "Just my

thanks," he said, "for making this great dinner."

He forked up some mashed puffs and beans and filled his mouth.

His mother looked at him. "Thank you, Arthur—I think."

She might have said more, but the phone rang. She jumped up to get it.

Saved by the bell, thought Arthur—at least **for now**.

After dinner, Arthur went to his room to do his homework.

*Think of a word that **rhymes** with* rope *and* hope.

"Arrghhh!" said Arthur.

He **switch**ed quickly to math. The first problem **involve**d cutting a **rectangle** in half.

"I wish I could cut that **envelope** in half," said Arthur.

Another question was about a **mailbag** filled with letters. There was no **mention** of the *E* word, but that was all Arthur could think about.

He began **doodling** on the **edge** of his paper. He started with a big rectangle, an **enormous** rectangle, the largest rectangle in the world.

*But was it only a rectangle? No, it was a giant envelope, and it was **chasing** Arthur down a hill. It **tumbled end over end**. Arthur could **barely** keep ahead of it.*

*"Don't run," the envelope was saying. "I know you'll **fit** nicely inside me. And don't worry. I will never let you out."*

*"No, thank you," said Arthur. "I'll get flattened." He ran faster.*

*"That's not my fault," said the envelope, **huffing and puffing**. "I'm just not in very good shape."*

Arthur **rubbed** his eyes. He needed a break.

He took a **peek** in Kate's room. She was already asleep.

"Babies are lucky," he **mutter**ed. "They don't have to worry about envelopes. Or **history** tests. Or summer school. They only have to look **cute** and fill their **diaper**s."

Kate turned in her sleep, and her **blanket slip**ped off her.

Arthur put it back. "The good old days," he **sigh**ed.

His mother was sitting in her office. She was **chew**ing on a pencil and **hum**ming while she worked. Arthur **tiptoe**d past the door. He found his father and D.W. watching *The Karaoke* ★ *Kitten*s show on TV.

The kittens were wearing **straw** hats and dancing **in a line** while they sang.

"Those kittens are crazy," said D.W. "Watch carefully now. This is the best part."

"How do you know?" asked her father.

---

★ **karaoke** 노래방. 본문에서는 '고양이 노래방 쇼'라는 TV프로그램 이름으로 나왔다.

Arthur sat down. "She's seen this episode eighty-four times," he explained.

"And it just gets better and better," said D.W. She shook her head **in time** with the music.

Her father hummed along. "Not every kitten can dance like that," he **point**ed **out**. "It takes a lot of **practice**."

A **commercial** came on.

*"Is the stress of everyday life **get**ting **you down**?"*

Arthur **nod**ded.

*"Do you feel like you're no longer in control?"*

Arthur nodded again.

*"The **pound**ing, the pounding. It just won't stop."*

Arthur **cradle**d his head in his arms.

*"For the chance to feel like your old self again, try Painfree or Painfree Plus. **Headache relief** is just minutes away."*

Arthur stood up. If only he could take a **pill** to **get rid of** his problem. But things were not that easy.

"You really look tired, Arthur," said his father.

"I am," Arthur **admit**ted.

"Sshhhh!" said D.W. "The kittens are going to sing '**Fur** Ball.' I love that song."

Arthur didn't stay to hear it. With a quiet "Good night," he went up to bed.

# Chapter 8

As Arthur got ready for bed, he found himself looking at his **pillow**. He had never **notice**d before how much it looked like a **stuff**ed **envelope**.

While brushing his teeth, Arthur brought his face right up to the mirror. His teeth lined up in little **square row**s.

Almost like envelopes, he thought.

Everywhere he looked—the **wallpaper**, the **carpeting**, the pattern on his **blanket**—he saw envelopes. They came in every **shape** and size.

"I **have** envelopes **on the brain**," he decided. "What I need is a good night's sleep."

Arthur climbed into bed and pulled up the covers.

"Are you still **awake**, Arthur?"

D.W. was standing in the **doorway**.

"No. I'm **sound asleep**. You're a bad dream. Go away."

"If you're sound asleep, how can you tell me to go away?"

Arthur sat up. "What do you want?"

"I want to know about the trouble you're in."

"There's no trouble, D.W."

She was not **convinc**ed. "What was in that mysterious envelope?"

"I don't know," Arthur said **honestly**.

"Mom didn't **mention** it to you?"

"No, she didn't."

"Oh." D.W. was **disappoint**ed. "Don't

worry. I'm sure you'll get in trouble for something else."

"Thanks, D.W. That makes me feel much better."

"Anytime," said D.W., and went back to her room.

Arthur **stare**d at the **ceiling**. **Strictly** speaking, he had told D.W. the truth. His mother *hadn't* mentioned to him what was inside the envelope. Of course, that was only because she hadn't *seen* it yet. The envelope was still sitting in the **wastebasket**.

Why can't it just stay there? thought Arthur.

He closed his eyes for what seemed like only a second.

*His eyes opened.*

*Arthur heard some paper* ***rustling***. *What was making that sound? He got out of bed and listened.*

*The sound was coming from* ***downstairs***.

Arthur followed the noise into the kitchen. The wastebasket was shaking—as if something was **bouncing** around inside it. Arthur looked down. Mr. Haney's envelope was growing bigger right before his eyes! The wastebasket could no longer hold it.

Arthur pulled the envelope free and ran upstairs. The envelope was **flap**ping in his arms. It was getting too big to carry. Arthur **drag**ged it along the floor to the bathroom. He **hoist**ed it into the **tub** and drew the shower curtain.

The curtain shook and **tremble**d.

Arthur screamed—and **fled** downstairs into his mother's arms.

"What's going on?" she asked.

Arthur **grab**bed her arm and pulled.

"We have to get out of the house, Mom. It's getting too big!"

As they stepped outside, one corner of the envelope **wriggle**d through a window. Another

PRIVATE
CONFIDENTIAL

**pop**ped out of the **chimney**.

"What's going on?" asked his mother.

"It's the envelope," **yell**ed Arthur. "Don't open it! It could be something **horrible**!"

At that moment the roof flew off the house. The top of the envelope rose up, and the flap opened.

D.W. popped out.

"You **trick**ed me, Arthur," she said. "You haven't even told Mom yet."

"Noooooo!" cried Arthur.

# Chapter 9

Arthur woke up. His hands were **cross**ed in front of his face.

"I can't go on this way," he **mutter**ed. "Even summer school would be better than this."

He walked **downstairs**. His father was still watching TV. It was some kind of cooking show.

*"Parsley, sage, rosemary, and thyme* may make for a good song title, but don't use them together as **seasoning**s."*

---

★ **parsley, sage, rosemary, thyme** 향신료로 쓰는 허브들. 파슬리, 세이지, 로즈메리, 타임.

"It might be **worth** trying," Mr. Read said to himself. "Maybe in a soup . . ."

Arthur kept going. His feet felt like **lead**, and his legs seemed to be moving in slow motion.

The **envelope** was still in the **wastebasket**. Arthur picked it out.

He walked over to the dining room, where his mother had her work area.

The light was still on.

Arthur took a deep **breath**. "It's going to keep **bother**ing me until I **get this over with**."

He entered the dining room.

"Do you have a second, Mom?"

His mother put down her pen. "For you, two seconds.★ But why are you up so late?"

---

★ **two seconds** 잠깐 시간이 있냐고 물을 때 "Do you have a second?"라고 하는데, 글자 그대로 보면 "(잠깐 내어줄) 1초(a second)를 가지고 있냐"는 뜻이다. 여기서는 이 말을 장난스럽게 받아서 "너한테는 1초뿐만이 아니라 2초(two seconds)도 내어줄 수 있다"고 답하고 있다.

TAX.

Arthur took a deep breath. "That's what I need to talk to you about. I **was supposed to** do something **right away** when I got home. But I was worried I might be in trouble, so I didn't do it, and now I'm afraid you're going to get mad—"

"Slow down, Arthur! What's going on? You can tell me. I won't get mad."

"Promise?"

She **nod**ded.

Arthur handed her the envelope. She **slit** it open and **glance**d inside.

"Ah! Here it is!" She **frown**ed. "Arthur, I've been waiting for this all night."

Arthur looked down at the floor. "You said you wouldn't get mad."

"Yes, yes, I did." His mother took a deep breath. "Well, I'm not mad **exact**ly. *Frustrated* would be a better word. I'm very frustrated. I've been trying to reach Herb for hours. I need this information."

"But this is from Mr. Haney."

"Herb is his first name.★"

She glanced through the papers.

"Um, Mom?"

"Hmmmm. . . . Yes, Arthur?"

"What's in there?"

His mother looked up. **"Tax document**s.
I'm doing his tax return.✳"

**"Nothing to do with** me?"

"Not unless you want to help Mr. Haney
pay his taxes!"

Arthur laughed. "Good-bye, summer
school," he **murmur**ed.

Mrs. Read put down her papers for a
moment. "Now I think I understand," she
said. "But Arthur, even if this was about you,

---

★ **first name** 이름. 지위나 관직에는 보통 성(last name)만 붙여 말하기 때문에,
아서는 엄마가 연락하려고 하는 Herb씨가 Harney 교장 선생님인지 모르고 있었다.

✳ **tax return** 소득 신고. 납세 의무자가 세법에 의하여 소득 신고서를 제출하는
행위.

we would need to know."

"What if it was something bad?"

His mother **sigh**ed. "**Put**ting **off** bad news doesn't make it get any better. And sometimes it makes it worse. Besides, Dad and I can't help you with a problem if we don't know you have one."

Arthur nodded. "I guess that's true."

"Well, we can talk more in the morning. Now back to bed, honey. It's late."

She gave him a kiss.

All that worrying for nothing, thought Arthur. He had **torture**d himself all afternoon and evening for no good reason.

"**Cheer** up, Arthur," said his mother. "You're not disappointed, I hope. Because if you really want to be in trouble, I'm sure I could **arrange**—"

"Good night, Mom!" Arthur said **hurried**ly, and **bolt**ed for the door.

It was too late for Arthur to call his friends, but he could imagine their **reaction**s.

"You're still alive?" Francine would say. **"Way to go!"**

Buster would be **please**d, too. "Now we'll be together all summer! If you get in any trouble then, I'll be right there beside you."

"Rats,*" Binky would say. "You got **off the hook** again? I can't believe it."

As Arthur was about to head up the stairs,

---

★ **rats** (속어) 젠장, 이런.

he saw D.W. waiting for him.

"So, tell me what happened!" she said. "Are you **ground**ed for a year? Off to **jail**? Can I have your room?"

"Back to bed, you two!" their mother called out.

"I'm just getting a drink," said D.W. She **stare**d at Arthur. "I'm waiting. . . ."

Arthur **shrug**ged. "Sorry to **disappoint** you, D.W., but there's nothing to tell. I don't know where you get these crazy ideas."

"Crazy ideas? Where do I get them?" She stopped to think. "Let me see. I wasn't the one **frozen** in **terror**. Or **jumpy** as a **frog**."

"Frozen? Jumpy?" Arthur's eyes opened wide. "What an **imagination**!"

"**Come on**," said D.W. "Tell me. Are you moving into the **garage**? Is Pal moving there with you? Are we—"

"Enough questions," said Arthur. "I'm not

telling you anything."

"You're not?"

Arthur smiled. "D.W., this is one mystery you'll have to solve on your own."

She **made a face** at him, but Arthur didn't care. He felt better at last.